the CRitter club

Ellie Steps Up to the Plate

by Callie Barkley ♥ illustrated by Tracy Bishop

LITTLE SIMON
New York London Toronto Sydney New Delhi

This book is a work of fiction. Any references to historical events, real people, or real places are used fictitiously. Other names, characters, places, and events are products of the author's imagination, and any resemblance to actual events or places or persons, living or dead, is entirely coincidental.

 LITTLE SIMON

An imprint of Simon & Schuster Children's Publishing Division • 1230 Avenue of the Americas, New York, New York 10020 • First Little Simon hardcover edition January 2018. Copyright © 2018 by Simon & Schuster, Inc. All rights reserved, including the right of reproduction in whole or in part in any form. LITTLE SIMON is a registered trademark of Simon & Schuster, Inc., and associated colophon is a trademark of Simon & Schuster, Inc. For information about special discounts for bulk purchases, please contact Simon & Schuster Special Sales at 1-866-506-1949 or business@simonandschuster.com. The Simon & Schuster Speakers Bureau can bring authors to your live event. For more information or to book an event contact the Simon & Schuster Speakers Bureau at 1-866-248-3049 or visit our website at www.simonspeakers.com. Designed by Laura Roode. The text of this book was set in ITC Stone Informal Std.

Manufactured in the United States of America 1217 FFG

10 9 8 7 6 5 4 3 2 1

Cataloging-in-Publication Data for this title is available from the Library of Congress.

ISBN 978-1-5344-1179-1 (hc)

ISBN 978-1-5344-1178-4 (pbk)

ISBN 978-1-5344-1180-7 (eBook)

Table of Contents

Chapter 1   Morning Music 1

Chapter 2   A Surprise Hit 13

Chapter 3   Lost and Found 25

Chapter 4   Paging Dr. Purvis 37

Chapter 5   Beginner's Luck 53

Chapter 6   Baseball Basics 67

Chapter 7   Eye on the Ball? 79

Chapter 8   All Eyes on Ellie 91

Chapter 9   Practice Makes Perfect 103

Chapter 10   Baby Steps 117

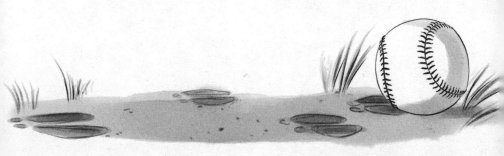

chapter 1

Morning Music

Ellie rolled over in her sleeping bag. She opened her eyes, blinked, and squinted. A shelf full of books came into focus. She read the titles on their spines:

Horses in Ancient Times

Speaking Your Horse's Language

100 Amazing Horseback Riding Trails

Ellie remembered where she was. She, Liz, and Amy had all slept over at Marion's house! It was one of their Friday-night sleepovers.

Ellie sat up and looked around Marion's room. Sunlight peeked in through the curtains. Marion still had her sleep mask over her eyes. Across the room, Liz was snoring. Amy was in a sleeping bag right next to Ellie's.

"Psssst," Ellie whispered into Amy's ear. "Are you awake?"

Amy stirred. But she didn't wake up.

Boring, thought Ellie. It was no fun to be the first one awake. She reached into her backpack. *I guess I'll use the time to practice my song.*

Later that afternoon, Ellie was going to audition for a solo in her youth chorus. She looked over the music and sang quietly to herself.

Out there in the dark,
I'm gonna let it shine. . . .

Ellie sang it over and over again. She closed her eyes as she sang. She imagined herself singing it perfectly for the choral director, Mr. Lewis. She imagined getting the solo! Then she imagined standing out front when the chorus performed the song at their next concert.

"*Let it shine, let it shine, let it shine!*" Ellie sang, putting some feeling into it.

Marion sat up in bed. "Does it have to shine so loudly?" she said sleepily.

Amy rolled over and opened one eye. "Yeah," she mumbled. "I was wondering that too."

Ellie clapped a hand over her mouth. "Sorry! Sorry! I was trying to sing quietly," she whispered.

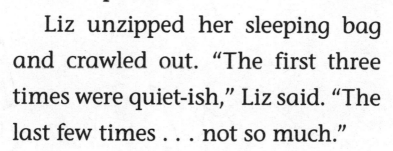

Liz unzipped her sleeping bag and crawled out. "The first three times were quiet-ish," Liz said. "The last few times . . . not so much."

"Oops," Ellie said sheepishly.

The four girls laughed.

"Well, we are all awake now," Marion pointed out. "So what's this song you're practicing?" She looked at the clock. "At seven thirteen? On a Saturday morning?"

Ellie explained excitedly about her audition later that day. "If I do well," she said, "I'll be a soloist at the concert next month."

Amy's eyes went wide. "The big concert at the Santa Vista Music Hall?" she asked. "The one that always sells out?"

"Yeah, that one!" Ellie exclaimed, clapping.

Marion sat on the floor. "I'd bet they get hundreds of people at that concert," she said. "That doesn't make you nervous at all, does it?"

Ellie shrugged. "Not really," she replied.

"Our fearless Ellie!" Liz said proudly. "Good for you!"

Ellie laughed. Being onstage just felt . . . exciting. She had always loved performing. The bigger the audience, the better!

A Surprise Hit

"So how did the audition go?" Liz asked Ellie at school on Monday. Their class was in line on the way to gym.

Ellie gave Liz a thumbs-up. "I think Mr. Lewis liked my audition," she said. "He even clapped at the end." She crossed her fingers. "He's going to announce the soloist at the next rehearsal on Saturday."

The gym teacher, Mrs. Payne, met the class at the gym door. "Hello, Mrs. Sienna's class!" Mrs. Payne said. "We're going outside today."

The class cheered. They loved having gym outside.

"I need a few helpers," Mrs. Payne went on. She handed out buckets of baseballs, bats, gloves, rubber bases, and orange cones.

"Baseball!" cried Joey, a boy in their class. "Yes!"

Ellie had never played baseball before. Not unless you counted Wiffle Ball on the beach with her family. She could hit the ball, for sure. "Keep your eye on it!" her dad would say before every pitch.

Ellie listened as Mrs. Payne gave them some pointers. They went over the rules of baseball. They did some throwing and catching drills with partners. They practiced hitting the ball off a tee.

Then Mrs. Payne divided the class into two teams. "Let's play a quick inning," she told them. Ellie's team would hit first. After three outs, they'd switch and be the fielding team.

Santa Vista Elementary didn't have a real baseball diamond, so Mrs. Payne laid out the rubber bases. She put out some orange cones to mark the edges of the outfield. "If you hit it over the cones, it's a home run!" she told them.

Then Mrs. Payne took her place as the pitcher. "Okay, line up, hitting team!"

The kids formed a line near home plate.

"You're up, Ellie!" called Mrs. Payne.

Ellie hesitated. *Me? First?* she thought. She looked around. How had she wound up first in line?

Everyone was waiting for her. So Ellie grabbed a bat. She stood at the plate and held the bat in position. She pretended she was at the beach.

She heard her dad's voice in her head. *Keep your eye on it!*

Mrs. Payne wound up. She let the ball go. Ellie locked her eyes on it. She swung hard.

Crack!

The ball jumped off the end of her bat. Ellie watched it as it soared up into the blue sky.

Chapter 3

Lost and Found

The ball kept going and going, over the heads of the infielders *and* the outfielders. It sailed over the orange cones! Finally it hit the grass. It bounced into some brush at the edge of the woods.

Ellie looked around. Everyone looked as amazed as she felt.

"Home run!" Mrs. Payne yelled.

"Run your bases, Ellie!"

Ellie was in shock as she rounded first base.

"Way to go!" cried Amy, the first baseman.

She ran past Marion at short-stop. "I didn't know you played baseball!" Marion said.

"Me neither!" Ellie replied.

Liz high-fived her at home plate.

"Nice job!" Liz cried.

The rest of their team crowded around Ellie, cheering. Lots of them gave Ellie pats on the back.

Mrs. Payne came over to congratulate her. "Home run on the first pitch!" she said to Ellie. "Do you play on a team?"

Ellie shook her head. "No. I've never played before," she said. "Just Wiffle Ball at the beach!"

Mrs. Payne laughed. "Well, you are a natural, then!" She turned to go back to the pitcher's spot, then paused. "You know, Ellie," she said. "Our after-school baseball league starts today. We have practice every day after school. You should

think about coming out." She looked around at the whole class. "Everyone is welcome. No tryouts. Just fun!"

Then Mrs. Payne asked Ellie to go find her ball. So Ellie jogged off toward the woods.

As she did, she imagined herself in a baseball uniform. She'd never thought of herself as an athlete before. *I guess it could be fun,* she thought. *Sort of like performing. But on a playing field instead of on a stage.*

Ellie got to the edge of the woods. She scanned the brush for the ball. She lifted long branches. She pushed leaves aside with her foot. She didn't see the ball anywhere.

So Ellie took a few steps into the woods. She stepped carefully, watching for poison ivy. *Leaves of three, let it be!* she thought.

Ellie peeked behind some birch trees. The ball wasn't there.

Ellie checked on the other side of a fallen log. No ball there, either.

She turned to head back. Maybe she'd have to tell Mrs. Payne she couldn't find it.

Just then Ellie spotted something white in a bunch of ferns.

Aha! She hurried over. She reached out and moved a large fern frond to one side.

Ellie gasped and froze.

It wasn't the baseball.

It was fur—a patch of short, white fur on a small baby deer!

chapter 4

Paging Dr. Purvis

Ellie took a slow step backward. She was worried she had scared the deer. But it made no move to run away. It lay completely still, peeking out of the ferns with big wide eyes.

"Oh, you poor thing," Ellie said gently. She looked around. "Where's your mama, little one?" she said.

"Are you hurt? Or sick?"

The deer's body was curled up in a ball, its legs tucked under. Ellie couldn't see any injuries, but . . .

I'd better go get help, she decided.

Ellie forgot about the baseball and ran back to Mrs. Payne. The rest of the class gathered around as Ellie described what she'd found.

A bunch of the kids wanted to go see the deer, but Mrs. Payne said no. "We don't want to scare it," she told them. "Plus, we need to be cautious around wild animals."

Amy raised her hand. "Excuse me, Mrs. Payne," she said. "My mom is a veterinarian."

Ellie nodded. Dr. Melanie Purvis was the best vet she knew. She helped Ellie, Amy, Liz, and Marion run The Critter Club, the animal rescue shelter they had started.

"Can we go to the office to call Dr. Purvis?" Ellie asked. "Maybe she can come take a look at the deer."

Mrs. Payne agreed that was a good idea. So Ellie and Amy rushed inside the school to the office. The principal, Mrs. Young, let Amy use the phone.

Fifteen minutes later, Dr. Purvis drove up to the school. Amy and

Ellie met her in the drop-off circle.

"So, where's our patient?" Dr. Purvis asked.

The girls led Amy's mother down to the field. Gym class was over, and Mrs. Payne had taken every-one inside. But the principal had

given Ellie and Amy permission to miss class to show Dr. Purvis where the deer was.

Ellie led the way into the woods. She stopped a few yards from the ferns and pointed at them.

Sure enough, the baby deer was still there.

Dr. Purvis went a few steps closer. But she didn't touch the deer. She crouched quietly, observing. After about a minute, she stood up.

"I think it's fine," Dr. Purvis said.

Ellie was surprised. But Amy spoke before Ellie could.

"Really?" said Amy. "But why is it just lying there? Can't it get up?"

Ellie nodded. "And why is it here all alone?"

Dr. Purvis smiled. "Actually, it's normal for a mother deer to leave her babies. They go off to look for food. But she'll be back."

Ellie knew Dr. Purvis was a good vet. But she was still worried. "Are you sure?" Ellie asked.

"Pretty sure," Dr. Purvis replied. "The baby seems calm and quiet. It knows it's supposed to stay put so its mother can find it again. That's why it's not getting up or running away."

That made sense, thought Ellie. "But isn't the baby in danger?" she asked. "It's so little and defenseless."

Ellie hesitated. She didn't like the

idea of leaving the baby deer alone in the woods.

"Why don't we come back and check on it," Amy suggested. "Maybe after school or tomorrow?"

Ellie nodded. That made her feel better. "We'll be back," she called out gently to the deer.

Then she followed Dr. Purvis and Amy out of the woods.

Chapter 5

Beginner's Luck

Ellie's parents both worked, so at home after school, her grandmother, Nana Gloria, was usually the first to hear about Ellie's day. Today it was all about the deer in the woods.

"Do you think we could go check on it later?" Ellie asked hopefully.

Before her grandmother could

answer, the phone rang. It was Liz.

"Are you going to join Mrs. Payne's baseball league?" Liz asked Ellie.

Baseball practice! This afternoon! Ellie had forgotten all about it. "Are *you* going?" Ellie asked.

"I was thinking about it," Liz replied. "If you go, I'll go."

Ellie thought it over. "It *was* fun hitting that ball today," she admitted. Then Ellie had a sudden realization. The baseball practice would be at the school field! "We could check on the baby deer while we're there!" Ellie practically shouted into the phone.

Nana Gloria agreed to drive them over and pick them up after practice.

"I'm glad you came!" Mrs. Payne said when they got there. "Let me introduce you to everyone."

Ellie and Liz waved to a few kids they knew from class—a boy named Andrew and two girls, Mia and Abby. There were also kids from the other second-grade class and a bunch of third graders.

"Did you bring gloves?" asked Mrs. Payne.

Ellie and Liz shook their heads.

"That's okay," Mrs. Payne replied. "I have a couple extra." She handed them each a glove.

Ellie looked around at the other players. They all had gloves. Did they all know to bring their own?

Then she noticed their shoes. Most of them were wearing special baseball cleats.

She looked down at her sneakers.

Ellie had that sinking feeling she got when she forgot her lines at play rehearsals.

"We'll start with batting practice!" Mrs. Payne said. "Everyone take a fielding position. I'll call you up one by one to bat."

Ellie and Liz walked to the outfield. They watched as Mrs. Payne pitched to the others.

Some were good. Abby hit some hard line drives. Andrew got a bunch of infield hits.

Others were great. Mia got three hits into the outfield. And a third grader got even more.

With each batter, Ellie got more nervous about taking her turn. But before long Mrs. Payne called her name.

"Ellie! You're up!"

Ellie looked over at Liz, who gave her a thumbs-up. Ellie smiled nervously and ran in from the outfield.

Oh well, she thought. *So what if everyone sees that I'm a beginner? I am a beginner.*

Ellie grabbed a bat and stepped into the batter's box.

The ball flew toward her. Ellie swung. *Clack!* She hit it off the end of the bat. The ball bounced toward first base. "Ooh!" cried Ellie, pleasantly surprised.

"Nice one!" said Mrs. Payne. She pitched another.

Pop! Ellie popped it up high enough to sail over the infielders' heads.

On the third pitch—*crack!*—
Ellie really made contact. The ball
soared toward Liz in the outfield.

Mrs. Payne threw Ellie nearly
two dozen pitches. She hit almost
all of them.

By the end, Ellie was giggling
with excitement. *This is the best
game ever!*

Baseball Basics

"Maybe Mrs. Payne is right," Ellie said to Liz after practice. "Maybe I really *am* a natural."

Liz laughed. "You sure looked like one today!" she replied. "Unlike me! Did you see all those strikes?"

The girls were walking toward the woods. They had a few minutes before Nana Gloria came to pick them up. They wanted to check on the baby deer.

Ellie took Liz to the spot where they'd left it. "Look," Ellie whispered, pointing into the ferns.

"Awww," Liz said softly. "It's adorable!"

Ellie agreed. "Dr. Purvis said to let her know if it was crying out," Ellie said. "Or lying stretched out on its side."

But the deer still seemed alert and calm. "I guess it's doing okay," Liz said.

Ellie smiled and nodded. "Let's come see it again tomorrow," she suggested. "We'll be here for practice every day this week."

On Tuesday the team did a lot of fielding drills. Some of the ground balls rolled between Ellie's legs.

And she had a tough time catching pop flies. She kept losing sight of the ball in the air.

"Oops!" Ellie giggled, slightly embarrassed, as a ball landed next to her.

On Wednesday they practiced
throwing to first base from different
points around the field. Ellie was at
third base. But she could only throw
the ball about halfway across the
diamond. Mrs. Payne moved her

to second. Even from there Ellie's throws bounced before the first baseman could reach the ball.

"Well . . . I guess my arm needs work," Ellie said to Liz.

On Thursday and Friday they

played practice innings. Mrs. Payne moved the kids around to try out different positions.

Ellie decided she was most comfortable in the outfield. She felt perfectly fine about the ball not coming her way very often!

"Our first game is on Saturday," Mrs. Payne told the team. "So let's make sure we've got the basics down."

She went over a lot of rules. But Ellie wasn't quite following everything. Mrs. Payne explained something called "tagging up" and

"overrunning first base" and what it meant to be in a "rundown." Ellie wound up feeling *more* confused.

At least they had batting practice every day. That was Ellie's favorite part. Hitting the ball hard and watching it fly made her feel better.

"I'm nervous for our game tomorrow," Liz said after Friday's practice. "Are you?"

Ellie thought for a moment. "Not really," she answered honestly. "My hitting isn't bad. And the rest is probably not as important. Right?"

But Liz didn't look so sure.

Chapter 7

Eye on the Ball?

Ellie ran onto the field, feeling like a real baseball player.

Their game was at the Little League baseball diamond in the town's park. It had actual white base bags. It had a backstop behind home plate. It had baselines marked with white powder. And it had a fence marking the outfield boundary.

Plus, Ellie was wearing her brand-new uniform. The team shirts were royal blue with white letters: *SVE* for Santa Vista Elementary. On the back was Ellie's number, 7.

How did they know my favorite number? That has *to be good luck,* Ellie decided when she saw it.

A small crowd had come out to watch. Ellie's mom; dad; grandmother; and brother, Toby, were there. Ellie saw Liz's family too—her parents and her big brother. They were sitting in lawn chairs behind the first baseline.

Even Marion and Amy had biked over to watch. Ellie waved to them from right field. They waved back. Amy gave a thumbs-up. Marion clapped encouragingly.

Right behind them, Toby cupped his hands around his mouth. "Don't mess up!" he called out loudly.

Ellie groaned. "Thanks a lot, Toby," she muttered under her breath.

The team from the Orange Blossom School was up first. Their leadoff batter, a tall girl, stepped into the batter's box.

"Play ball!" the umpire shouted.

Please don't hit it to me. Please don't hit it to me, Ellie thought. She got ready. She held her breath with every pitch. Three swings and three misses later, the batter was out.

Phew! Ellie thought. *Two more outs and we'll be up!*

But the second batter hit a single. Then the third batter hit a grounder

toward first base. The first baseman
fielded it and stepped on the bag.
The batter was out. But the other
base runner had made it to second
base.

"Two outs!" announced the
umpire.

The next batter swung hard at

the first pitch, but missed. The next three pitches were balls. Uh-oh! One more ball and the batter would walk.

What happened next seemed to go in slow motion.

The pitcher wound up. The ball flew. The batter swung.
And the ball sailed.

The first baseman jumped, reaching up into the air. But the ball was too high! It went flying high over his glove. As the first baseman landed, he turned. He looked into the outfield—at Ellie.

Oh no! The ball was coming her way!

Ellie took two steps forward. She took two steps back. Where was it going to come down?

Maybe right on her head!

Ellie closed her eyes, ducked— and raised her glove in defense.

Thwap!

She felt the weight of the ball in her glove. She froze. Had she really caught it?

Chapter 8

All Eyes on Ellie

Ellie looked up—just in time to see the ball roll out of the glove. It fell with a *thud* onto the grass.

"No!" she cried out. In frustration, Ellie threw her glove onto the ground.

That's when she noticed her teammates yelling from the infield.

"What?" Ellie called back. She

couldn't make out their words. Then
Ellie saw that Toby was yelling too.
"I know, I know!" she shouted. "I
messed up."

"No!" Liz called from center field.
"The ball! Pick it up! Throw it to the
infield!"

The Orange Blossom baserunners were running around the bases!

In a flash, Ellie picked up the ball. She threw it as hard as she could. But it got only halfway to the pitcher.

And then it was too late. Both baserunners had scored.

The numbers on the scoreboard changed.

Ellie knew it was her fault.

Even though Ellie had a tough game, it wasn't *all* bad. She batted three times. And she got on base twice with two great hits.

But both times she made base-running errors.

The first time she was running from first to second. She overran second base. The second baseman had the ball and tagged her out.

The second time she forgot to run when her teammate got a hit. They both wound up on first base. Ellie got tagged out again.

In the end it was a close game. Orange Blossom won by one run.

"Good effort!" Mrs. Payne said in their team huddle. "We came up short this time. But we'll learn from this game and be stronger next week."

Ellie looked around at her teammates. Some of them seemed dis-
appointed. But they were good
sports. They all nodded at what

Mrs. Payne said. Then they high-
fived one another as they said their
good-byes.

Mia and Andrew even patted
Ellie on the back. "Not bad for your
first game!" Mia said.

Ellie forced a smile. They were
being so nice. But she felt terrible.

She walked over to Mrs. Payne.

"Thank you for giving me a chance," Ellie said to her. Her bottom lip trembled a little bit. "But we lost today because of me. I'm not a natural, after all." She handed Mrs. Payne her glove. "Sorry, Mrs. Payne. I shouldn't be on the team."

Ellie turned and hurried away.

"Ellie! Wait!" Mrs. Payne called to her.

"Come back, Ellie!" Liz shouted.

Ellie kept walking. All she wanted was to find her family and go home.

Practice Makes Perfect

Unfortunately for Ellie, she couldn't go home.

In the car, her mom reminded her about youth chorus rehearsal. The baseball game had gone long. There wasn't even time to stop home to change.

Ellie groaned.

Then, with a sudden thrill, she

remembered that Mr. Lewis was announcing the soloist today!

Baseball—what was I thinking? Ellie thought. *I'm no baseball player. I should have stuck to the stage in the first place. That's what I'm good at.*

In the rehearsal room, Mr. Lewis stood up in front of the chorus. Everyone took their seats.

"First things first," Mr. Lewis said. "Thank you to everyone who auditioned for the concert solo. Many talented singers gave it their

best. But I chose one. That person
is . . . Ellie Mitchell!"

Ellie gasped.

"Ellie, congratulations!" exclaimed
Mr. Lewis.

All around her, kids were clapping. Ellie beamed, her smile light-
ing up her face.

What a day she was having. This definitely made up for the baseball game.

Mr. Lewis asked everyone to get their music out. But Ellie just sat there in a happy daze. She was picturing her name in the printed concert program. *Featured soloist: Ellie Mitchell.*

She didn't hear a word Mr. Lewis was saying. Not until the whole chorus stood up and began to sing. Then Ellie jumped to her feet and hurriedly opened her music folder.

When rehearsal was over, Ellie stuffed her music away. She couldn't wait to tell her parents about the solo!

But as she got up from her seat, she dropped her folder. All the sheet music fell out.

Ellie sighed and bent to pick up the pages.

As she did, she overheard two girls talking in the row near her.

"You're not quitting, are you?" one girl asked the other.

Ellie's ears perked up. Quitting? Someone was quitting the chorus?

The other girl answered gloomily. "Yeah, I think so." She sighed. "I guess I'm just not a singer."

Ellie popped up and turned around. "Oh, don't quit," Ellie told her. Her name was Katie. She had a beautiful alto voice. Her spot on the concert risers was right behind Ellie's. So Ellie knew her voice well. "You are *definitely* a singer!"

Katie smiled. She looked a little embarrassed that Ellie had over-heard what she said. "Thanks,"

111

Katie said. "But this was the fifth solo I auditioned for. I haven't gotten a single one."

Ellie nodded sympathetically. She knew she'd feel frustrated by that too. "Maybe you just need practice at *auditioning*?"

Katie shrugged.

"Do you get nervous at auditions?" Ellie asked her.

"Oh yeah," Katie replied. "I definitely do."

So Ellie gave her some audition tips. She told Katie how she practiced the song until she could sing it in her sleep. She sang it to herself in the mirror. She sang it for anyone who would listen. Sometimes she asked Nana Gloria to record her singing it. Then Ellie listened to see what needed work.

"By the audition," Ellie said, "everyone is a little sick of the song. Even me."

Katie laughed. "Wow," she said. "You prepare a lot. No wonder you got the solo." Katie smiled. "I'll try those things next time."

Ellie clapped. "So you're not quitting?" she asked.

Katie shook her head.

"Good," said Ellie. "A little practice can go a long way!"

As she said those words, Ellie realized: She should take her own advice.

Baseball.

She had to give it another try.

Baby Steps

After school on Monday, Ellie, Liz, Amy, and Marion walked out of Santa Vista Elementary together.

"So you're coming to baseball practice later?" Liz asked Ellie hopefully.

Ellie nodded. "Yes," she said. "You think Mrs. Payne will take me back?"

Liz smiled. "Of course she'll take you back!" she said. "She didn't want you to quit in the first place!"

"Hey," said Marion. "Do you think the team needs a manager?" she asked. "I might come today and ask Mrs. Payne."

"Yes!" Ellie cried excitedly. "Marion, you would be the best

manager." She turned to Amy. "Now you have to join too! Then we'd all be on the team together!"

Amy hesitated. "I don't know," she replied. "But I was thinking that it might be fun to report on the games for the school paper."

"Perfect!" said Liz.

"There's just one thing," Amy went on. "I'll need to learn the rules a little better."

Ellie laughed. "So will I," she said. "It's okay. We can learn them together."

Just then Liz gasped. She pointed toward the ball field. "Look!" she cried.

Ellie looked where Liz was pointing. "Oh my!" she cried out in delight.

Across the field, on the grass at the edge of the woods, were two deer—one big and one very small. The larger deer nudged the baby with her nose. The baby took one wobbly step forward. Then another. Then a few more.

"Awww," Amy cooed. "It's still a little unsteady on its feet."

"Yep," said Ellie. "But it'll be off and running in no time." She looked at her friends and smiled. "All it needs is a little practice. And I know all about practice!"